The Donkey and the Garden

Green Bean Books

First published in the Hebrew language in Israel in 2019 by M. Mizrahi Publishing House
First published in the UK in 2021 by Green Bean Books
c/o Pen & Sword Books Ltd
47 Church Street, Barnsley, South Yorkshire, S70 2AS
www.greenbeanbooks.com

Paperback edition: 978-1-78438-637-5
Harold Grinspoon Foundation edition: 978-1-78438-641-2

Designed by Ian Hughes
Edited by Kate Baker and Phoebe Jascourt
Production by Hugh Allan

Printed in China by Printworks Global Ltd, London and Hong Kong
042135K1/B1629/A6

FSC
www.fsc.org
MIX
Paper from
responsible sources
FSC® C129961

The Donkey
and the Garden

Devora Busheri

Illustrations by Menahem Halberstadt

This is the story of Rabbi Akiva, one of the most influential scholars in history. He was a great rabbi and a wise leader, and his name was known far and wide. Even today, we speak of Rabbi Akiva and his many important lessons passed down through the generations.

But this story isn't like other tales. It doesn't start at the very beginning when Akiva was small. Instead, it begins when he was big. In fact, when he was all grown up . . .

Once upon a time, Akiva was all grown up. He had a wife named Rachel. He had a job as a shepherd. And he had a house – well, maybe not quite a house, but a barn full of straw that kept the two of them warm in winter and gave them shade in summer.

Rachel had left a home full of riches to be with Akiva.
Akiva knew that although he was poor and didn't even
know how to read or write, Rachel believed in him.
He hoped that one day they would have a better life.

One morning, Rachel and Akiva went for
a stroll. They passed pretty flower beds,
vines with ripe grapes, and a little house
where children were learning to read and write.

"Wouldn't you like to go inside and learn how to
read with them?" asked Rachel. She knew that
even though Akiva was forty years old and
big and strong and wise, he was sad that
he couldn't read or write.

Akiva looked down at the small children running past his feet. "Can you see anyone here who is as tall as I am?" he asked Rachel.

"I am a shepherd," he reminded her. "When I stand tall, I can see where each and every little lamb of mine has wandered." Towering high, he chuckled. "I think they might laugh if I try to squeeze myself onto one of their tiny benches."

The next morning, Rachel called Akiva out into the garden.

"I want to show you something," she said. "It's a donkey. But not just a regular donkey . . . It's a donkey with a garden on its back." "A *garden* on a *donkey*?" Akiva was bewildered. "Yes," said Rachel. "This is a special donkey."

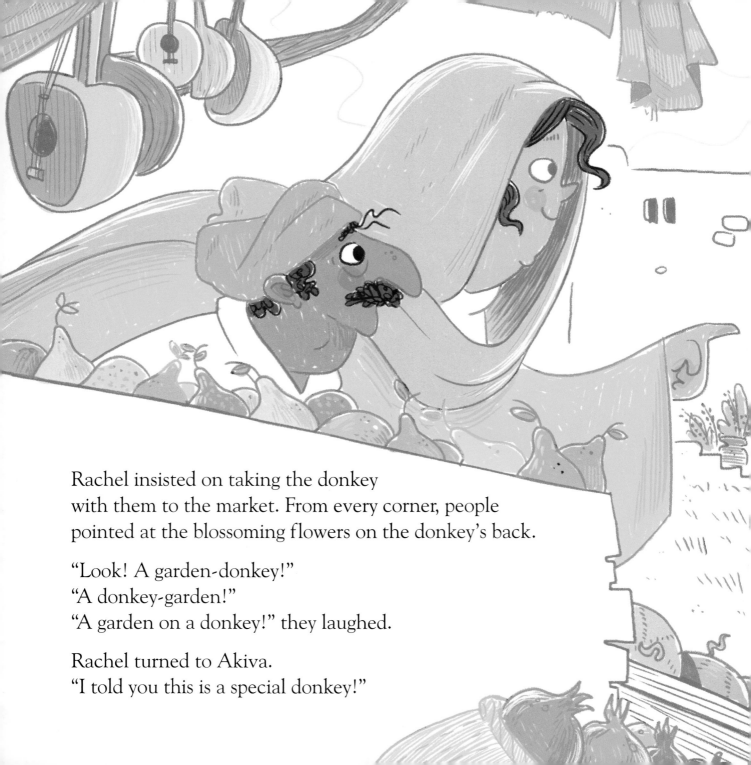

Rachel insisted on taking the donkey
with them to the market. From every corner, people
pointed at the blossoming flowers on the donkey's back.

"Look! A garden-donkey!"
"A donkey-garden!"
"A garden on a donkey!" they laughed.

Rachel turned to Akiva.
"I told you this is a special donkey!"

The next day, Akiva and Rachel once again walked past the classroom full of children.

"Won't you just give it a try?" asked Rachel.

Akiva gazed in awe at the wondrous letters on the writing board, but then looked down at himself. "Do you see anyone in there with such big hands?" he asked.

"I am a shepherd," he reminded her. "If one of my sheep is weak or one of my lambs is looking for its mother, I can pick it up with my strong hands, like so." And he swept his animals up into his arms. "Everyone will laugh when they see the pen disappear into my enormous palm."

Rachel smiled. "If you don't want to go to school," she said, "will you come back with me to the market?"

"With the donkey?" asked Akiva.
"Yes, the very same donkey," laughed Rachel.
"The one with the garden on its back!"

Again, they went to the market, and again
everyone laughed and pointed:
"A garden-donkey!"
"A donkey-garden!"
"A garden on a donkey!"

On the third day, Rachel suggested once again that Akiva go to learn with the children. Again, he refused.

"Well, the garden on my donkey is looking lovelier than ever this morning . . ." said Rachel.

"So it will draw even more attention in the market today," said Akiva. And off they went.

Indeed, the garden was beautiful. It blossomed and bloomed with flowers and fruits and berries.

But this time, no one at the market shouted, "Garden-donkey!" or "Look at that donkey!"

A little girl came by and plucked a ripe purple grape from the donkey's back. A young boy cut some plant stalks and made a bracelet for his sister. An old man picked a red flower for his granddaughter's hair.

"I think they've gotten used to it," said Akiva.

"I think they like it," said Rachel. Akiva and Rachel both laughed. Suddenly, Akiva understood what Rachel had been trying to tell him.

And so, from that day on, while Rachel looked after the sheep on her own, Akiva went to school.

On the first day, he was nervous and tried to hide his long legs between the benches.

On the second day, he sat hunched over his work,
his pen disappearing into his huge hand.

On the third day, a little boy asked Akiva to help him hold the heavy aleph bet board.

"Such a big man," said the boy with wonder. "Such clever children," thought Akiva.

On the fourth day, he wrote
his very first letter.

On the fifth day, he wrote
his first word.

Many days
went by,
and Akiva
continued
to write and
learn . . .

ואהבת לרעך כמוך

. . . until, finally, he became a true scholar. He knew how to interpret every letter of the Torah. He became a rabbi and a leader, and his name was known to the people of his generation. In fact, his name and teachings – including **'love your neighbour as yourself'** – are still known to this day.

"Once upon a time, when I was all grown up, I learned how to read the Torah."

"Once upon a time, when I was all grown up, I learned how to speak Hebrew."

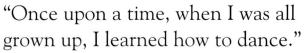

"Once upon a time, when I was all grown up, I learned how to dance."

"Once upon a time, when I was all grown up, I learned how to ride a bicycle."

"Once upon a time, when I was all grown up, I planted a garden."

"Once upon a time, when I was very small, I learned how to . . ."

MIDRASH HAGADOL

When Rachel, wife of Rabbi Akiva, encouraged him to study, he said: They will laugh at me, for I am forty years old and know nothing. She said: I will show you something wonderful. She brought forth a donkey and threw dirt on its back and planted a garden. She said: Take him to the market. The first day they laughed at the donkey; the second day they laughed at him; but on the third day they didn't laugh any more. She said to Akiva: Go study Torah. Today they will laugh at you, tomorrow they will laugh at you, but on the third day they will say: that's just the way he is. Akiva went and studied with his own son. He held a board on one side, and his son held it on the other. They wrote Hebrew letters on it, and Akiva learned them.